After Sto

By

Eddie D. Moore

Contents

Terry of Medina, TN	3
Nick of Phoenix, AZ	4
Prisoner Four	11
Chad of Roswell, NM	16
Loose End	21
Shanghaied	22

Terry of Medina, TN

I couldn't choose between my 12 gauge and my .270, so I put them both in the trunk with the ammo. It took me nearly fourteen hours to get to Denver. After checking into a crappy Motel 6, I crashed for the night with my Ruger under my pillow. I still had an eleven-hour drive ahead of me the next day, so I had to be up early.

I would've been there to rush the gates of Area 51 with everyone else if it hadn't been for that flat tire. At least I was there to help the survivors regroup.

Nick of Phoenix, AZ

Nick glanced at the handcuffs securing his arms to the table, balled his fists, and let out a long sigh. The hairs on his arms stood up, and he shivered. The room's only air vent was directly above his chair. He glanced at the block walls and then stared at his reflection in the two-way mirror in front of him.

The door opened, and NCIS agent Tolman took his usual seat, back to the mirror. He took a sip of his coffee and asked, "Are you comfortable, Nick? Can I get you anything?"

"I'm not stupid, Agent Tolman. If I ask for my jacket back, you're just going to turn the heat back on until I'm ready to ask you another favor. I'm sure your coffee is just one more temptation for me to place myself at your mercy, and increase my awareness of how dependent I am on you."

Agent Tolman didn't blink or acknowledge Nick's accusations. "Do you want some coffee?"

Nick rolled his eyes. "Yes, I'd like a cup of coffee and these handcuffs removed. It's not like I'm going anywhere. There's no telling how deep under Area 51 you've taken me."

"Oh, I'm not offering to take off the cuffs. You can drink your coffee through a straw. You managed to get past armed guards, and undetected by the military's most advanced proximity sensors to gain access to a highly classified area. Until I know how you did it, those cuffs are staying locked tight."

"I've already told you how I got here."

Anger crept into the agent's voice. "Do you have any idea how many people died last night? If it were up to me, I'd have you put in front of a firing squad, no matter how small your part in all this! So, how about you start again."

Seconds passed as the agent stared into Nick's eyes. The door opened and a uniformed woman curled her upper lip as she placed a cup of coffee on the table. Nick glanced at the cup and wondered what she might've done to the drink before taking a sip.

Agent Tolman clicked his ink pen and picked up his notepad, "I'm ready when you are."

Nick sighed and began telling his story for the third time. "I came for the party. A couple of friends decided at the last minute to come along, so we rode our Harleys all the way here from Phoenix."

"Are you a member of a gang?"

"No, we just ride for fun. The campgrounds here had tents full of beer and live music. There were even tents set up with topless dancers. All three of us took vacation time to make the trip.

Anyway, after a dozen or so beers, several people thought it would be a blast to approach one of the roadblocks and say hi to the troops. Everyone was drunk and happy, but the soldiers were not amused. They ordered us back and pointed a couple of water cannons in our direction.

A representative of the group stepped forward and tried to explain that we just wanted to say hi, but his words were cut short by 20 liters of water per second. He fell to the ground and tumbled back towards the group. Things kind of escalated into chaos from there."

Agent Tolman shook his head. "You expect me to believe that you had no intention of actually storming past the gates."

Nick ground his teeth. "I came on my Harley with two changes of clothes. My bike is sitting beside my tent, and my clothes are in the saddlebags. Don't you think I would've come better prepared if I had planned on actually doing it? When you find Greg and Dennis, they'll confirm that much of my story."

"If they're still alive, I will ask them."

Nick asked with concern and a hint of disbelief, "What do you mean if they're still alive?"

"Please continue."

After a short pause, Nick relented. "Okay, a couple of guys ran forward to help the fallen man, and they got knocked down as well. When the second water cannon let loose, dozens of people rushed forward as if they had a point to prove.

I took the opportunity to slip away and followed the fencing for a couple of hundred feet. That's when I found where the fencing had been cut. I could just make out by the moonlight three dark figures crawling on the ground on the other side of the fence.

The guards were distracted, and people were flocking towards the shouts of the group confronting the roadblock. So, I decided on a whim to follow the guys that had cut through the fence. I've never so much as received a speeding ticket, so I figured what were they going to do, give me a fine and a slap on the wrist? It'd make a great story for my grandkids one day."

The NCIS agent rolled his eyes. "They could've shot you."

Nick's eyes dropped, and he shrugged. "I did mention that I was drunk, right?"

"You ever heard of federal trespassing? Do you consider six months in jail a slap on the wrist?"

Ignoring the agent's questions, Nick continued. "The guys I followed were focused on moving forward. They never noticed that I was following. When they reached a row of parked vehicles, I eased over to the edge of a building and slipped behind a dumpster. I saw one of them hold his hand against the egress keypad beside the large hangar doors."

"Did he have anything in his hand?"

"No, he just placed his hand on the pad."

The NCIS agent didn't appear convinced. "Hmm. Which hanger was that again?"

Nick let out a breath in a huff. "Twelve. For the third time, it was hanger twelve."

Agent Tolman scribbled another note and nodded. "Continue."

"A few seconds later, the door opened and all three of them slipped inside. All I wanted to do was grab a souvenir to prove that I had made it onto the base and get the hell out of there, so I ran to the door half expecting it to be locked, but to my surprise, the keypad was dead and the door opened when I pulled.

Look, if you need me to sign something saying that I won't talk about what I saw inside that hanger, I'll do it. I know how to keep my mouth shut."

Agent Tolman raised an eyebrow. "I'm just here to get to the bottom of what happened. You'll have to take that up with your attorney if you get one."

"What do you mean?"

"You engaged in rebellious and treasonous acts against your country. You could spend the rest of your life on a tropical island in the Gulf of Mexico."

Nick blinked. "That doesn't sound too bad."

The investigator shook his head. "I'm talking about Gitmo, Guantanamo Bay, you idiot."

"Oh." Nick swallowed the lump in his throat and took a sip of his coffee that had grown cold. "There was a spaceship inside the hanger."

"How do you know it was a spaceship?"

"I've seen enough science fiction movies to know a spaceship when I see it."

"Okay, what happened next?"

"I saw around a dozen or so people run up a ramp under the ship to get inside. The three men I followed into the hangar were the last to enter the ship. A few seconds later, the ramp withdrew and the ship began to hover a few feet off the ground. The hanger doors opened, and the ship inched its way through the opening.

Bullets ricocheted everywhere bouncing off the ship, and I dove for cover behind a couple of large wooden crates. I peeked out just as the ship opened fire on the aircraft sitting on the tarmac. I saw one of the other hangers explode, and a high pitched whine vibrated the air. A moment later, the spaceship became a streak of light that shot into the sky.

I watched dumbfounded as the ship became a dim speck in the distance. I never even noticed the soldiers surrounding me. The next thing I knew my face was smashed into the concrete floor and someone bound my hands and feet with zip ties."

Agent Tolman nodded. "Lucky for you, your story is consistent." He raised his right hand and curled his fingers twice. An instant later, two large men wearing desert camouflage entered the room.

One of the men unlocked the cuff on Nick's left hand, and his hopes rose as he stood up that this ordeal might be about over. Nick's hopes fell when the soldier twisted his arm behind his back and reattached the handcuffs.

Agent Tolman scribbled down another note and said, "Take him to Dr. Dorden for memory cancelation."

Nick struggled as the soldier led him out of the interrogation room and shouted over his shoulder, "What do you mean by memory cancelation?"

"Don't worry. When you wake up tomorrow, you won't remember the last three days, and the doctors will probably tell you not to drink so much in the future."

Prisoner Four

"Guard!" Thad rested his head against the bars while he waited. He heard the guard's footsteps approach.

"What do you want, prisoner four."

Thad sighed. "I want you to call me by my name, but I'll settle for a trip to the infirmary. My head is killing me."

"Where do you think you are? A grade school campout? This is a top-secret military prison for ungrateful treasonous soldiers who are no longer worthy of name or rank. I'm not unlocking that door for a headache."

"I've told you before that none of us are from this planet. I'm telling you something is wrong. I need to see a doctor, now!"

The guard eyed the sweat on top of prisoner four's shaved head and hesitated. His voice wasn't as confident when he replied, "You just told me that you're from another planet. How am I supposed to believe anything you say?"

Thad began to shake uncontrollably, and a moment later, he crumpled to the floor in a violent seizure. Foam and spittle dripped from his mouth as the guard fumbled for the keys and shouted for help.

"Clark, grab a stretcher! Newsome, call the infirmary and let them know that we've got one coming their way!"

The prisoner in the adjoining cell shouted, “The man tried to tell you he needed help!”

“Shut your mouth, five!” The guard shouted.

One of the inmates further down the cellblock yelled at the guard sent for the stretcher, “Run, fat boy! Run!”

The prisoner opposite Thad’s cell stood at his door and watched silently as the guard opened the door and went inside. The guard held two fingers against Thad’s neck and glanced up.

“Have a seat, twelve. I don’t like being stared at.”

Prisoner twelve nodded his head a fraction of an inch when Thad cracked open an eye.

Thad sprang into motion and kicked the guard’s feet out from under him. He moved with unnatural speed and had the guard wrapped into a chokehold before he could cry out. Thad snatched the keys from the guard’s hand and tossed them across the hall.

“Move, Davon! The clock is running.” As Davon worked to unlock his door, Thad raised his voice. “Most of the base is distracted by the idiots camped outside! Our ship is repaired and waiting in the hanger! I plan on leaving this rock behind tonight! Who’s with me?”

Shouts of agreement ran up and down the cellblock. Davon managed to get two other doors unlocked before the guard returned with the stretcher. The guard’s eyes went wide, and he turned to run, but one of the other prisoners jumped him before he could take three steps.

Thad lowered the unconscious guard to the floor, and shouted, “Don’t kill anyone unless we have too!” He glanced back at the guard on the floor before leaving his cell, and said in a lower voice, “It’s not their fault they chose to lock us away.”

Thad snapped, “Lark! Tulsi!” Two women looked in Thad’s direction. “Clear us a path to the hanger. As soon as you’re close enough for your implants to connect, shut down the proximity sensors.” The women jogged out of the cellblock.

Once all the doors were unlocked, Davon approached Thad and nodded. “We spent a hundred years in cryo to get here, and we’re just going to take the ship and leave?”

Thad sighed. “Would you rather spend the rest of your life locked away down here and studied?”

“No, they’ve made it quite clear that they don’t feel that we can be trusted. We’re all with you. But where will we go?”

“We’ll figure that out once we’re in orbit. Maybe we’ll just go home.” Thad raised his voice. “I managed to send a message to the rest of our squad a couple of weeks ago. If everything has gone according to plan, they’ve created a distraction and should be waiting for us topside. Davon, take the lead. I’ll follow to make sure no one lags behind. Now, let’s move!”

As the last of the squad, filed out of the cellblock, Thad stopped to check on the guard that brought the stretcher. He shook his head and closed the guard’s eyes. He found two more bodies at the nurse’s station and his anger flared. He jogged to the next teammate in line.

Thad tapped him on the shoulder, and when he saw his face, he said, “Brown, make sure no one falls behind.”

Brown nodded, and Thad jogged to the front of the line. He caught up with Davon at the base of the stairs that lead up and into the hangar.

“Davon, I said no killing unless it was necessary.”

“They were dead when I found them. I guess Lark & Tulsi didn’t agree with your no-kill policy. Honestly, I don’t think any of us do.”

Thad took a deep breath. “And what if another ship is sent here?”

“Then maybe they will treat their next visitors with more respect. Besides, anyone we left behind could have compromised our escape. Some of us are beginning to wonder if you are willing to do what needs to be done to get us out of here.”

Thad knew what Davon wanted to hear, what his team needed to hear, but after coming with peaceful intentions, it felt like a failure. “We’re going to do whatever is necessary to get off this planet. I don’t have a problem with that.”

Davon stared into Thad’s eyes for a moment, nodded, and then glanced up the stairway. “They’re on the ship.”

“Good.” Thad grimaced like he had just swallowed something distasteful. He ascended the stairs two at a time and glanced around the hanger before motioning for the others to follow. “Everyone on the ship!”

The three expected squad members joined the others and boarded the ship. Thad noticed a man hiding behind a few sealed crates, decided that he wasn't a threat, and joined the others on the ship.

Chad of Roswell, NM

"I'd like to welcome everyone to the Pearson and Green podcast. We're broadcasting from an undisclosed location. We're going to call our guest today, Chad, to protect his identity. Chad, thank you for meeting with us today."

Chad glanced at the narrow basement windows before answering. "Thanks, as long as you guys weren't followed, I'm glad to be here."

Green chuckled. "How do we know that *you* weren't followed?"

The expression on Chad's face tightened. "If I had been followed, they would've shut us down before we started broadcasting."

Pearson cleared his throat. "Chad was attending the festivities near Area 51 last week and witnessed the tragedy that occurred there."

"That was no tragedy. It was a freaking massacre, guys. Everything you see on the news is one giant cover-up."

"Do you have any evidence that the government is covering up what truly happened?" Pearson asked.

"The complete lack of evidence is your proof. I saw the alien ships destroy the planes on the ground, and I was in the middle of the tent city when they turned their attention on the rest of us, but the official story is terrorism.

Who were the terrorists? Where did they get their weapons? Who funded them?"

As Chad paused to light a cigarette, Green leaned closer to the microphone and said, "There are at least twenty witnesses that tell a different story."

Chad took a long drag and blew the smoke Green's direction. "How many people developed a case of amnesia that night?"

Pearson shrugged. "There were 436 people killed that night and at least that many severely injured. I think whatever happened there was traumatic enough to justify a few cases of repressed memories."

"Repressed memories." Chad laughed. "I know two people that saw the same things I did, but they hung around to help. One of them swears on his mother's grave that he slept through the whole thing, and the other claims to have seen the terrorist cutting through the fence and infiltrating the base. The sad thing is that they both actually believe they're telling the truth."

Green raised an eyebrow. "Why didn't you stay to help, Chad?"

"What was I going to do? I couldn't put out the fires, and my pistol wasn't going to do anything to the spaceships. I can guarantee you half of the people listed as dead were actually abducted. I saw the beams of light that pulled them into the ships. I heard their screams for help, but there was nothing I could do."

"So, you made a run for it," Green said.

A flash of anger colored Chad's face. "Of course, I made a run for it. It was total chaos." Chad pulled a few photos out of his jacket pocket and handed them to his interviewers. "Look at these snapshots. Once I felt like I was a safe distance away, I stopped long enough to take a few pictures."

Green and Pearson looked over the photos. Pearson selected the best image and spoke to the audience. "Ladies and gentlemen, I can see the tents burning in the distance and a few lights in the sky. Chad, are these lights spaceships?"

"Yes."

"Why are they so blurry?"

Chad rolled his eyes. "Have you ever seen a clear image of an alien spacecraft?"

Green laughed. "No, I don't think anyone has. Maybe that's because aliens don't exist."

Chad's eyes narrowed. "Or their propulsion system distorts the electromagnetic spectrum so that you can't get a clear photo."

Pearson held up hands and cut in. "Hold on guys, we're all here for the same reason to make sure the truth goes public. After all, that was the spirit behind the whole Storm Area 51 movement." Chad and Green visibly relaxed. "Chad, there are dozens of witnesses out there that contradict your story. Most blame the tent fires on poor planning and a windy night. They also point out that those who attended the event provided a distraction for the terrorist to sneak onto the base."

Chad shook his head. "I've been researching the backgrounds of these witnesses." After handing Pearson a folder, he continued. "Look these over. If you haven't noticed, the major news networks tend to interview the same five or six people, and I'm pretty sure that two of them weren't even there."

Green gave Chad a skeptical look. "What evidence do you have that they were never there?"

"Both of them have posted on social media nearly every day for years but neither one of them posted anything on September 19th or the 20th. They were supposedly attending one of the most popular events of the year, and they were both completely silent about it? Don't you think that's a bit odd?" Chad glanced at his phone to check the time, but when he looked back up, his expression left no doubt that he was alarmed.

Pearson glanced at Green before asking, "Is there something wrong?"

Chad swallowed hard and lowered his voice. "I had cell service when I came down here."

Green glanced at his computer screen. "It says we're still connected."

Chad glanced at the narrow basement windows and tensed when he saw feet running around the building. He stood up when he heard footsteps descending the stairs. A man with slicked black hair, a goatee, a dark suit, and a smug grin was the first to appear. Two large men with guns in hand followed a step behind the man wearing the suit.

The man in the suit glanced around the basement, nodded to one of the men following, and sighed. "Don't be alarmed. No one is going to hurt you." The man he nodded to leaned his head and mumbled something into a microphone.

Chad took a step back. "Who are you?"

Four people wearing scrubs descended the stairs carrying briefcases, and the dark-haired man sighed. "I'd introduce myself, but none of you will remember me in a couple of hours anyway." He shook his head and said, "I think I'll just save my breath this time."

Loose Ends

Dr. Chapman had just finished setting up his equipment and programming the computer when Agent Holman entered the room. Even after working with the agent for months, the doctor still hadn't gotten used to the man's commanding presence. Dr. Chapman forced himself to smile as he greeted him.

"Good afternoon, Agent Holman. I got your email this morning. I understand your investigation is coming to an end."

The Agent didn't return Dr. Chapman's smile. He never did. "Yes. This will be our last memory alteration, and then you will be free to move on to your next project. Is everything ready?"

Proud of his work, the doctor nodded and pointed to the start button. "Just one push of the button and your witness will forget everything that has happened for the last six months and two weeks. All we need is the patient."

"How long have we been working on this project, doctor?"

Dr. Chapman counted the months on his fingers. "I'd just got home from a cruise when I got the call that my services were needed. It's been around six months." The doctor's eyes widened as Agent Holman pointed a pistol his direction.

"Have a seat, doctor."

Shanghaied

Lewis sat up without opening his eyes and groaned as he rubbed his head and face with both hands. His skull felt like it was about to split open and spill his brains onto the floor. The mattress he sat upon felt unfamiliar and thin, so he slowly opened his eyes and lifted his head.

The walls were completely white and unadorned in the small cabin. He shook his head in confusion but stopped as a wave of nausea rose in his throat. The coveralls he wore still had the lubricate stain on the left leg from his last shift, and the last thing he remembered was going for a drink after finishing the repairs on that salvage ship. He racked his brain trying to remember the name of the woman that had offered to buy him a drink. As the name came to mind, the cabin door opened, and Marlene stood on the other side.

"It's about time you woke up. The captain is expecting you."

While clutching his head, Lewis asked, "The captain? How did I get here?"

"You don't remember joining the crew last night?"

Lewis looked up too quickly and winced. "Join the crew? I wouldn't do that; I love working maintenance on the Callisto Space Station. Spending all your time on one spaceship would be like getting married and sleeping with the same woman day after day. I'd go crazy!" He paused for a second, and his eyes widened. "Where are we?"

Marlene brushed back her red hair and rubbed her neck. “We left space dock shortly after you retired, about ten hours ago. Sol is just a bright pinprick behind us by now. Sometimes you just have to make the best of a bad situation.”

The color drained from Lewis’ face. “Make the best of a bad situation! You’ve got to be kidding me. I need to get back to the Callisto.”

“Like I said the captain wants to see you. You can take that up with him.” Marlene motioned for Lewis to follow and walked away.

Even with a splitting headache and a stomach that threatened to empty itself at any moment, Lewis couldn’t keep his eyes from straying to Marlene’s backside. He forced himself to pick up the pace for a few steps and catch up with her.

“My head is killing me. How much did I have to drink last night? I only remember two.”

Marlene shrugged as she stopped in front of the captain’s office. A plaque beside the door read Captain Bill G. Brown the Notorious. Lewis raised an eyebrow as he read the nameplate. Marlene cleared her throat and smiled before saying softly, “It was a gift.”

As the doors opened, Captain Brown looked up. “Ah, Lewis. I’ve been waiting for you. You slept well, I hope? Have a seat. You have no idea how glad we are that you’ve chosen to join us.”

The cushion in the chair Lewis sat in sank several inches forcing him to slightly look up at the captain. To his surprise, Marlene also sat down in the captain’s office. Her chair seemed to have held her up fine, and she sat with her back straight.

"Look, Captain, there has been some kind of mistake here. I need to get back to the Callisto ASAP."

The smile slid off the captain's face. "I'm afraid that would be impossible. Do you know how much it would cost in fuel to decelerate and go back now? Not to mention the time we'd lose."

"I love my job, and I've never had any desire to do any kind of work out here in the black. Everything I need and want in life is on that space station. There's nothing out here to do but watch remastered holo-vids and perform preventive maintenance."

The captain let out a long slow breath and waved Marlene's general direction. "Mr. Martin, Marlene here is our Procurement Specialist. It's her job to make sure this ship has all the supplies and manpower required to complete our next job. Our engineer retired when we docked for repairs, so she approached you with a job offer. I have here a contract signed by you accepting those responsibilities. Maybe you should take the time to look it over; it offers a very generous compensation package."

Lewis glanced at Marlene and ground his teeth. "I think someone drugged me last night, and if you just take me back now, I won't press any charges."

A hint of outrage tinged the captain's voice. "That's a serious accusation, Mr. Martin. Do you have any evidence to support that claim?"

Lewis opened his mouth to answer but closed it a second later.

Since no answer was forthcoming, the captain continued. “I will admit that you were a little intoxicated during our interview, but I chose to ignore that for two reasons. One, we don’t carry alcohol on this ship because an emergency could occur at any moment. Our lives depend on each other out here, and I expect every member of this crew to be ready to act at all times.

Secondly, we needed someone immediately. We couldn’t afford to sit around on our hands waiting for the right person to come along, so I chose to overlook the possibility that you might have a drinking problem. The people we asked said that you were the best and could repair anything, so Marlene approached you with the offer. It’s not anyone’s fault here if you can’t hold your liquor.”

Lewis held up a forestalling finger, but the captain ignored it.

“Mr. Martin, your request to turn this ship around is denied, and I see no reason to believe that our Procurement Specialist has done anything illegal. If you don’t like it here, you can resign when we return to the Callisto Space Station. Until then, I expect you to perform your assigned duties. Do I make myself clear?”

Lewis worked his jaw from side to side as he thought through his situation. He had no doubts that he had been shanghaied. But what could he do about it? After ten hours, anything they drugged him with would surely be out of his system, so there’d be no physical evidence to give the authorities. It appeared his only choice was to go along with their ruse until they docked somewhere that he could catch a ride back to Callisto.

Lewis let out a long resigned sigh and nodded. "You can count on me. I'll keep the ship operating at peak efficiency. Can I ask where we're going?"

The captain studied Lewis' face for a long moment and then visibly relaxed. "You look like crap. Marlene will take you to see Daniel. He's the closest thing we have to a doctor. We'll meet in the conference room in about an hour and go over our mission plan."

Marlene stepped out of the captain's office, and as Lewis followed, the captain added, "Oh, and you might want to give the slide drive a once over. We'll be using it right after the mission briefing, and I'll consider your first day a success if we aren't vaporized."

Lewis nodded and followed Marlene until they reached a name plaque stamped sickroom. Marlene pointed to the door and said, "Daniel will be inside. I'm sure you can find the control room on your own. I've got a few things to take care of before the mission briefing."

Lewis glanced at the door and then paused to watch Marlene walk down the corridor. Just as he turned to open the door, Marlene shouted over her shoulder. "You better get moving. The captain doesn't like it when people are late, and stop ogling my ass."

Lewis took a breath to protest her accusation, but a second later, Marlene took a sharp right down a side corridor. He waved his hand in front of the sensor under the nameplate, and the doors flew open and rebounded several inches before finally staying open.

A man wearing shorts and a Hawaiian shirt jumped and held out an arm as if to block whatever was about to attack him before dropping into a chair. "You must be our new engineer. I sure hope you can fix that door. It scares the crap out of me every time."

Lewis stepped in and the doors slammed shut behind him. After a glance around the cramped room, he extended a hand and said, "You must be Daniel? While I'm at it, I'll change that plaque out there to say 'sick closet.' Someone was exaggerating when they called this a room."

Daniel gave Lewis' hand a quick shake and then sanitized his hands. "It's nice to meet you, Lewis. Yeah, I know your name. News travels fast among a small crew. What can I do for you?"

"I've got a hangover the size of the Tarantula Nebula."

Daniel tapped at an interface on the wall and three tablets dropped from a dispenser. "I've been there a few times myself. These should do the trick. There's water in the mini-fridge."

"Thanks, I need to get a look at the slide drive before the meeting." Lewis didn't feel like getting to know these people, but he knew that he could be stuck with them for weeks, and as far as he knew, Marlene was the only one responsible for his current situation. "Maybe you can tell me about the ship and crew afterward. Give me an idea of what to expect."

"Sure thing."

Lewis popped the pills into his mouth, drank the entire contents of the water bottle, and grabbed a second bottle to take with him. He jumped when the sickroom doors slammed closed behind him even though he was expecting it. Adjusting the doors went to the top of his repair list.

After fifteen years and repairing thousands of spacecraft, Lewis had no problem finding the control room for the slide drive. Most ships followed the same basic design and looked like a large straw with a toothpick suspended in the middle. For decades ships were spun to create the centripetal force that gave the crew a sense of gravity. Gravity plating eliminated the need to spin the ship, but most manufacturers found that it was cheaper to keep building the same designs.

A fusion drive is used to accelerate the ship to twenty-two thousand kilometers per second and then the slide drive can take over. The math and physics in the operation of the slide drive were beyond even Lewis' understanding, but you didn't have to know how it worked to operate or repair a slide drive. The computer's diagnostics revealed what needed to be replaced, and in most situations, repair bots are deployed to do the actual work.

The inherent danger in operating a slide drive is making sure it doesn't get too close to any large gravitational masses and has enough fuel to reach its destination. Ships that got too close to a planet or sun tended to vanish. The slide drive cannot be shut down after a slide has been initiated, and if a drive depletes its fuel before the slide is complete, the resulting subspace implosion will destroy anything within ten kilometers.

Lewis expected to find technicians scurrying from workstation to workstation in preparation for the pending slide. Instead of a busy team, he was greeted by silence. A faint tapping caught his attention, and he found a dark-haired man with ear gauges the size of his thumb tapping a finger against the console and banging his head to the music in his headphones.

When Lewis touched the man on the shoulder, he jumped out of his seat and pulled off his earphones. “Man, you scared the crap out of me!”

Lewis held out a hand. “I didn’t mean to scare you. I seem to be doing that a great deal today. My name’s Lewis.”

“I’m Jason.” He eyed Lewis’ outstretched hand and took a step back. “For future reference, don’t touch me. I hate that.”

“It appears that I’m the new engineer.” Lewis motioned around the room. “Where’s the rest of the team?”

Jason laughed. “We’re it; we’re the whole team.”

“I think every ship I’ve ever seen docked had at least seven technicians in engineering.”

“Yeah, did you happen to notice the empty corridors on your way here?”

“Yes, but I didn’t think much about it. I’ve never actually left the space station.”

Jason paused the music that was playing loud enough for both of them to hear clearly. “We’re a mining and salvage operation. The smaller the crew we carry the more our profit split is off each job.”

“So, how many are on the crew?”

Smiling, Jason held up an open hand. “Five.”

Lewis shook his head in disbelief. “Five! This ship could man a crew of twenty.”

“Which would you rather have one twenty-fifth of a share or one-sixth?” Jason saw the confusion on Lewis’ face. “The ship always gets a portion of the profits.”

“The captain wanted… Why are you laughing?”

“Don’t call Bill Captain. It’ll go straight to his head and none of us will be able to tolerate him.”

Lewis blinked. “Okay, Bill wanted me to make sure we were ready for our next slide.”

Jason shrugged. “All the tanks are full. We can reach anywhere within fifty light-years and still have enough fuel to slide home.”

A view screen flickered to life. Lewis and Jason both turned as the captain spoke. “Ah, I see our new engineer found his way to the control room. You guys ready down there?”

Jason stretched and yawned as he answered. “Of course, we’re ready; you just need to tell me where we’re going so that the computers can calculate the slide.”

The captain nodded. “I’ll tell you that in the briefing room in ten minutes. Don’t be late.”

The screen went dark, and Jason took off his jacket revealing two arms covered in tattoos. “Let’s wait just a couple more minutes before we go.”

“Why?”

"Because arriving just on time for these mission briefings irritates the crap out of Bill, and he can't say anything about it because you're not late." Jason held out his arms. "These tattoos also drive him crazy. That's why I always take my coat off before these meetings."

"You seem to go through a great deal of trouble to irritate him."

"Nah, it's no trouble. I think of it as part of my job. Trust me you don't want him thinking he has everything under control." Jason glanced at the chronometer on one of the computer displays. "All right, let's go, but walk slow."

As they strolled through the corridors, Lewis realized that his headache was gone and that his steps seemed lighter. As he entered the conference room, a wave of dizziness washed over him, so he dropped into the seat next to Daniel, who was wearing an even more colorful shirt. The colors seemed to swirl together each time Lewis blinked.

Daniel leaned over and asked, "Feeling any pain?"

"No, but the room keeps wanting to spin now. What the hell did you give me?"

A mischievous grin spread across Daniel's face. "You're welcome."

The captain gave the chronometer and Jason's tattoos a glare tinged with irritation and stood up. "I know you aren't going to like this, but we are going back to sector 7a."

The air thickened with disapproving sighs and groans. Marlene was the first to find words to express her feelings.

"What the hell is wrong with you? You promised that we wouldn't risk that again!"

Jason used his arms to cushion his head on the table and mumbled, "This is it; we're all going to die."

The captain held up both hands as if he could physically hold their resistance at bay. "Listen to me this is the kind of job we've always dreamed about. Pull this job off and we can each have our own personal island in New Zealand for retirement."

Jason sat up and huffed, "Or we could fall helplessly into the gravity well of that white dwarf."

"I'm not going to let that happen, Jason."

"What are you going to do, get out and push? We were lucky to get out of there…"

Marlene cut in as a thought struck her. "This is why Wayne left, isn't it?"

The captain worked his jaw as though he were chewing something distasteful. "We discussed the possibility of making a return trip, and he agreed that the plan I have is possible, but he had already built himself up a nest egg large enough to live comfortably. He wanted to get out while he could."

"You mean he wanted off the ship before you left for this suicide mission." Marlene gritted her teeth and turn to face Lewis. "Welcome aboard. If I had known this was his plan, I wouldn't have… Well, you wouldn't be here. Sorry."

Lewis started to shake his head, but a fresh wave of dizziness made him stop. "Would someone like to fill me in? What happened in sector 7a?"

Jason opened his mouth to answer, but the captain beat him to it. "Four months ago, one of our survey probes reported a large metallic source orbiting a dwarf star. The probe was too far away to give any details. We expected to find a large iron-rich asteroid." He tapped an icon on the display built into the conference table and a hologram appeared. "We found this."

The hologram slowly rotated. It took a moment for Lewis to process what he was seeing, and his mouth dropped open as rationalization coalesced in his mind and he searched for the words that seemed to run away from him.

"That… That's not of human construction. We've never built anything like that." He pointed to a section that was obviously damaged in an explosion. "This damage appears to be very old."

Marlene sat back, rolled her eyes, and said with a voice full of sarcasm, "I told you that I found a genius."

The captain ignored Marlene. "The ship's sensors collected this image a few moments after we disengaged the slide drive and emerged in sector 7a."

Daniel slipped a pill out of his pocket and swallowed it. "And then we all almost died."

The captain grimaced. "We were hit by some kind of electromagnetic burst that burned out many of our systems. We spent the next two weeks free falling through the star system, and if it hadn't been for the skills of our engineer…"

"If it weren't for Wayne, we might not have broken free from that white dwarf's gravity well." Marlene made eye contact with Lewis for a brief second. "Our engineer wasn't the only one that decided to seek gainful employment elsewhere after facing death in sector 7a."

Daniel checked the pockets on his Hawaiian shirt for another pill and sighed when he discovered that they were all empty. "I would've left too, but I don't have anywhere else to go."

The captain's mouth drew slightly to one side. "And we all appreciate your dedication. Look, guys, I understand your fears, but think of the payoff we'd receive upon our return to Sol. The alien technology in that hunk of junk is worth more than I can count, and we're not leaving without it."

The room fell silent while those sitting around the table exchanged glances. Lewis could read the wordless argument that passed around the room by facial expressions alone. Marlene appeared to feel betrayed or perhaps hurt that the captain didn't entrust her with his plans. Daniel inspected his fingernails and only glanced up to make sure no one was staring at him. The determined expression on the captain's face never wavered.

Lewis looked the hologram over again and broke the silence. "Did the electromagnetic wave originate from the derelict?"

The captain shook his head. “I think it was some kind of mine.”

Marlene folded her arms. “As far as we know the whole thing is one big trap.”

“A trap for whom?” Lewis asked. “We could drop out of our slide a safe distance away, send in a probe to make sure there are no mines and get a better look.”

While shaking his head, the captain zoomed out the view. “It would take us weeks for a probe to travel that distance. We don’t have the time.” He glanced at Marlene and continued. “We have to assume that word of this discovery might have leaked out and that others are coming to claim our prize.”

Marlene’s face reddened. “Wayne promised that he wouldn’t tell anyone about this.”

“I don’t have any reason to doubt Wayne’s word, but he’s not the only person that recently left the ship. Just the location of this ship will be worth money, and even though we did our best to keep it a secret, we have to assume that someone may have figured out that we weren’t telling the rest of the crew that we found something here.”

The captain paused, and when no one objected, he continued, “I suggest that we leave the slide drive on until we are practically on top of it.”

Jason laughed. “That sounds like a great way to commit suicide. That’s way too close to the star for the slide drive.” He turned to face Lewis and waited for the engineer to back him up.

When Lewis finally spoke, a faint voice in the back of his mind whispered, *you're an idiot.* "We could do a timed and structured shut down on the slide drive. If we reduce the power to the drive as we got closer to the sun, it would dramatically reduce the danger, theoretically anyway."

Jason turned to face Marlene. "Genius? You found us a freaking mad man, Marlene."

"Just last month, I worked on a freighter that used the same procedure to shut down their drive when it became unstable. If they managed it with a drive that was failing, I believe we could do the same with a drive that's operating within normal parameters."

After fingering the gauge in his right earlobe, Jason nodded to himself. "But they didn't do the procedure near a sun, did they?"

"Well, no…"

Jason slapped the table. "Do you both have a death wish or something?"

The captain switched off the hologram and sank into his seat. "Let's give Lewis a chance to explain."

"Jason is right that just switching the drive off as you suggested would never work. The best analogy I can think of is that of a comet that's heading straight into the sun, but just before it gets there, it boils away leaving nothing left. There is a strong attraction between our drive and the sun while at full power, but as we power it down, that attraction will be proportionally reduced. It's just a matter of timing."

The captain and Jason stared at each other for several seconds before Jason looked away and said, "Yeah, the computers can calculate and time the shutdown, but I'm not saying this isn't risky."

Lewis nodded. "We might get shaken about quite a bit, but this ship is structurally stronger than the freighter that managed to pull it off."

After a long sigh, Marlene rolled her eyes and nodded. "Fine. I can see I'm outnumbered here, but if we all end up on the same side of eternity, I'll make sure that each one of you regrets it."

The captain smiled triumphantly and nodded to Lewis and Jason. "How long will it take to program the computers?"

"About half an hour," Lewis said.

The Captain glanced at a chronometer and nodded. "Perfect. You guys better get busy. I think you'll find that we have a slide window coming soon."

Marlene was the first to march out of the conference room, and Daniel quickly followed her. Jason mumbled to himself as they walked back to the control room. Lewis could only make out a few words Jason mumbled, none of which were very pleasant. Just before the control room doors closed, Lewis heard the sickroom doors slam open and Daniel curse.

Jason pushed his tattooed arms through his jacket and laughed. "Whatever you do, don't fix Daniel's doors."

"Why not?"

"He doesn't like to trip by himself, so every once in a while, he'll slip something into your drink if you aren't paying attention. He did that to Wayne once before a slide. When Wayne figured out what happened, he set the doors to slam open and shut to irritate Daniel." Jason chuckled to himself. "Wayne would often walk down the corridor and open the sickroom doors just to scare Daniel and kill his buzz."

"I thought the captain…"

Jason dropped into his seat and spoke over Lewis. "I told you he isn't our captain. I'd go so far as to say that *leader* is even too strong a word, organizer would be a little more accurate." He motioned to the chair next to him. "Have a seat, Mr. Engineer; it's time to earn your share on this excursion into the black."

Lewis swiveled the chair and jumped back as a calico cat landed at his feet and dashed across the room. "That is the ugliest cat I've ever seen in my life," he said as he sat.

Jason chuckled. "You'll get used to him." He pointed to the screen. "This is where the derelict was when we left, and here is where the computer calculates its position to be now."

Lewis shook his head. "I hoped that we'd have a little more time to work on this, but we're going to need to work quickly." While Lewis typed rapidly at the interface, the cat rubbed against his ankles. He spoke without taking his eyes from the screen. "It appears that I've made a new friend."

"You must be special. I've never seen him take to anyone else that quickly."

Lewis grinned. “Maybe he’s figured out that he’s too ugly to be choosy.” He finished typing and sat back while the computer projected their path and incorporated the shutdown protocols. He grimaced as the cat climbed into his lap and made himself comfortable. The computer chimed a soft tone when the program finished.

“Crap! We have less than seven minutes to engage the drive to hit the optimal window.”

Jason shrugged. “I don’t know about you, but I’d like to have the highest odds of success possible.” He activated the ship’s comm. “Buckle up people. We’ll be engaging the slide drive in five minutes.” He switched off the ship-wide and shook his head. “How did Bill of all people know that we were approaching our slide window?”

“I’m guessing, your previous engineer made the same calculations we did.”

“That makes sense.”

The skin between Lewis’ eyebrows furrowed. “Since the ship was hit with an electromagnetic wave last time, maybe we should shut down everything not needed for the slide.”

Jason nodded and began shutting down systems. “This is going to be strange.”

“How’s that?”

“You know, dropping out of a slide inside the solar system and cutting out weeks of sub-light travel. I just hope Bill doesn’t plan on making this standard procedure.”

“I thought the plan was for this to be the crew’s last flight or mission.”

Jason barked a laugh. “Trust me. It’s not the first time any of us have heard that promise. It’s best not to get your hopes up. You never know what’s going to happen out here.”

“Our total travel time should be less than an hour, but it could take us weeks just to figure out what to salvage.”

With less than a minute left on the count down, Jason put the cat into a padded kennel and buckled himself into his seat. The lights dimmed as the countdown fell below twenty seconds. A warning chimed the final five seconds, and when the clock struck zero, reality slipped away.

No one enjoyed using a slide drive. Second to fuel, the sanity of the crew is one of the largest limiting factors to how far a ship can travel. Most people describe the use of a slide drive as having your mind run through a blender. Thoughts, events, and dreams tended to get all mixed together. The mind tries to help by filling in gaps and creating new experiences that are often disorienting.

Lewis’ delusions became a disconnected, half-remembered tangle of thought. The ship jarred when the first power cut in the shutdown program took effect. Somewhere in his mind, he realized that drool was dripping from his chin. As he raised his arm to wipe it away, several power cuts happened in rapid succession. The drool was replaced by a flow of warm blood. The cat howled in its cage, and Jason moaned. The disorientation suddenly stopped and silence filled the ship.

“Are you okay?” Jason asked softly.

Lewis glanced at the blood soaking into his shirt and worked his jaw a couple of times before speaking. “Yeah, I must’ve bitten my tongue. You?”

In answer, Jason flipped the communication switch. “Are the rest of you still kicking? It looks like we lived down here.”

As the others announced their status, Jason went to check on his cat, and it bolted out of the cage as soon as the door opened to find a hiding place it considered safe.

The captain asked over the comm. “Why don’t I have any sensors?”

Lewis answered. “We shut down everything we didn’t need for the slide. They should be up and running in another minute or so.”

“Hurry up! We’re flying blind up here. I don’t want to run into the damned thing.” The comm switched off and immediately came back on. “Okay, the sensors are back online. Get your butts up here. We’ve got work to do.”

Lewis’ head still swam as they headed toward the bridge, and he wasn’t sure if it was a result of the slide or whatever Daniel had slipped him. He still couldn’t believe how fast his life had changed. One minute he was deeply entrenched into his daily routine, and the next he was pretending to be a willing part of the crew that abducted him. He bit his bottom lip at the thought. Letting his emotions show would do no good, and besides, maybe he was wrong and did drink too much before signing that contract.

The bridge was larger and more high-tech than Lewis expected, and he paused after stepping through the doors. Workstations lined the walls, and a single view screen filled most of the wall opposite the door he had just walked through. The derelict filled the screen.

Jason dropped into a chair. “Oh man, I’m going to need a screenshot of that ship when we’re done; I’ve got a bare patch on my left shoulder that needs some ink.”

The captain was watching Marlene pecking away at her workstation, and he looked up long enough to frown at Jason before turning his attention back to the screen. Lewis couldn’t hear the captain and Marlene’s discussion, but after a short exchange, the captain nodded and turned his direction.

“There is a section of that ship that’s still holding air pressure, but there’s no airlock to give us access to that area of the ship.”

Marlene shouted, “Look at this,’ and the display changed on the view screen.

“Looks like satellites or some kind of probes,” he tilted his head in thought, “maybe a sensor array?”

Lewis shook his head, “No, look at how they’re dispersed. I think they’re the source of the electromagnetic wave that crippled the ship on your first visit.”

The captain nodded slowly. “An automated defense system, I see it now. It looks like the ship took damage during a fight, and they got stranded here, so they deployed defensive measures. We have to assume that they called for help. Is there any way to tell how long ago that was?”

A cold chill ran down Lewis' back. "I've got a few other questions."

The captain raised an eyebrow and turned to face Lewis. "What?"

We got past their defenses by sliding in here." Lewis's shoulders lifted a couple of inches. "We can't power up the slide drive this close to the sun. How are we going to get past them to get home?"

"We have weapons."

Frustration crept into Lewis' voice. "We don't know their capabilities or how they will respond when attacked."

The captain let out a long slow breath. "There should be a way to shut them down on the ship."

Lewis laughed. "Do you people think we live inside of a cheap budgeted holo-vid episode or something? This is alien technology. We don't even know how they interfaced with their computers. We will not know how to read their writing, assuming they even used writing. Their computers could be controlled by thought or speech that we couldn't articulate even if we knew it.

"You're the engineer. I have no doubt that you'll figure it out."

"I get the feeling that you think I'm going to take one look around that ship and say, oh here's the off switch for the defenses, and then point out the most valuable pieces to salvage."

Daniel rested a hand on Lewis' shoulder and smiled when Lewis looked his direction. "I don't think you understand. If I know Bill, he's not planning on leaving anything behind."

Lewis waited for the captain to correct Daniel. The captain turned to stare at the display without refuting Daniel's suspicion. Lewis shook his head. "Oh, come on. You've got to be kidding me. That thing is huge."

A fire burned in the captain's eyes when he turned and snapped, "We'll take it in pieces if we have to, but I want it all if we can get it. We've towed asteroids to smelting facilities; I don't see why this should be any different!"

Lewis blinked. "And how much did those asteroids weigh? That ship is likely ten times bigger than anything you've handled before. We'd empty our fuel tanks just trying to reach slide velocity."

The captain opened his mouth, but Marlene cut him off. "How about we board the ship and have a look around before we argue about how much of it we can salvage." Lewis and the captain nodded to each other and Marlene continued. "I'm detecting some signs of power usage within the pressurized section, and I've found a place we can latch on to the hull and cut our way inside."

The captain rubbed his forehead and nodded. "Match velocity and latch us on." He made brief eye contact with Jason and Lewis. "You two drag the plasma torch to the extendable dock. I'll cut through myself if I have too."

Lewis grimaced and said, "Okay," before following Jason.

#

The extended dock latched to the side of the alien ship just as Jason and Lewis rolled the plasma cutter around the corner. The captain was waiting with a pile of EVA suits at his feet. The pressure indicator went from red to green, and the captain opened the door. Cold air poured out of the airlock and a thin layer of frozen moisture appeared on the surface of the exposed ship.

Bill rested a gloved hand on the hull and took two slow breaths before a smile spread across his face. "Suit up and drag the plasma cutter inside. The air over there might not be breathable."

As Lewis pulled on his suit, he asked, "What if the atmosphere is explosive?"

The captain stopped, glanced at the hull and back to Lewis. "Well then you can consider your contract fulfilled, and you'll be free to seek more fulfilling opportunities elsewhere."

Jason laughed. "I have no idea what the job market looks like on the other side of the pearly gates. Hopefully, we won't find out."

Marlene checked everyone's suits before pulling her helmet over her head. After Daniel checked her seals and gave her the thumbs up, she closed the airlock door. "Light it up, Jason, and make us a door."

The plasma torch flared to life with an audible pop. Jason narrowed the flame and held it a fraction of an inch away from the alien hull. A red spot appeared almost instantly and a second later turned white. Lewis noticed the others were holding on to handholds, so he did likewise.

When the torch punched through the hull, Jason stepped to the side. The captain held a sensor over the hole a moment and then nodded. “The air is breathable, but keep your suits on anyway.”

While they waited for Jason to finish cutting through the hull, the tension among them was replaced by an eager anticipation. With an experienced hand, Jason kept his cut a couple of inches away from the dock’s seal. As the torch’s path reached its starting point, Lewis unconsciously held his breath until the cut section of hull fell away and landed with a clang inside the ship.

The captain’s eyes twinkled as he stepped through the hole. “We appear to have gravity boys and girls. Let’s go see what treasures await us.”

The interior of the alien ship was a complete mess. Loose panels hung from the ceiling, and debris littered the floor. They passed half-open blue doors that were without a doubt crew quarters, but the captain didn’t spare any of the cabins much more than a glance as they marched toward the copper-colored door at the end of the hallway.

The copper doors opened as they approached, and on the other side, they found dozens of cylinders with markings down the side. Lewis ran his fingers over the slanted writing. “It looks alien to me.”

One end of the cylinders was topped with an opaque glass cap. Daniel touched the glass, and a light came on inside the cylinder. The glass cap became transparent, and Daniel cleared his throat. “So, these are aliens? I have to admit that I’m a little disappointed.”

Marlene lightly tapped the glass cap. "Look at the shape and size of his ears. They're a little smaller than normal."

As lights began to flash and spin inside the cryo-unit, everyone took a step back. The captain turned away with a sigh and blankly stared at the next unit in line.

Lewis stepped a little closer to the captain and asked, "What's the matter?"

"I was hoping to pick up the ship and get out of here, but this is a sleeper ship which means it doesn't have FTL capabilities. Even if it's alien, it's all old tech as far as we're concerned, and our aliens look too much like us to impress anyone." The captain shook his head. "And I've never turned a profit from a rescue mission. We can't just leave the people here."

Lewis nodded. "I'm glad to hear that I haven't signed on with heartless pirates. If it makes you feel any better, there's still a great deal of money to be made here."

The captain raised an eyebrow. "How's that?"

"Look at that writing, these people can't be from Earth no matter how human they look. This is a first contact situation. We're about to make history. The media networks will let each one of us name our price for an exclusive interview. Hell, the vid rights alone would be enough to make this endeavor profitable."

The captain perked up and nodded. "You're right. We can make history and play the heroes on this one."

They turned as the cryo-unit broke its seal with an audible decompression and a section retracted to let the occupant out. The man inside yawned, and anger flashed in his eyes when he noticed the suited people watching him.

The captain unlatched his helmet and removed it. He held up an open hand and said softly, “Easy, we’re not going to hurt you.” He placed his hand on his chest. “My name is Bill”

An automated alert flashed across Marlene’s vision, and she tore off her helmet. “The ship’s computers were just remotely accessed! We’re being hacked!”

“Not my ship!”

The captain took two steps closer to the cryo-unit but froze when the man shouted, “Stop! Don’t make me kill you and your friends!” After a few silent and tense seconds passed, he warned, “Don’t test me.”

The captain’s eyes narrowed. “We came here to help you. And the first thing you do is threaten the lives of my crew? What are you doing to my ship?”

“My name is Thad.” He tapped the side of his head. “Thanks to my implants I now have access to all the information on your computers. We came to Earth with peaceful intentions 85 of your years ago. They ended up keeping us all prisoners. Apparently, we weren’t the only ones. When we escaped, we detected several other ships leaving Earth right behind us.”

Lewis shook his head. “That’s not in any of our history books. Whether or not we’re alone in the universe is still a highly debated subject.”

Thad laughed without the presence of mirth. “It was made quite clear to us that humanity treasured their isolation and considered themselves our superiors even though we were the ones traveling between the stars. I think our ship was attacked because anyone that bothered to calculate our origination point would discover that we left from Earth."

The captain took a step back and mumbled, "Cyborgs. So much for playing the hero."

Thad lifted an eyebrow. "It seems that your kind hasn't lost its sense of superiority."

Daniel eased closer to the captain's side, swallowed a pill while everyone was staring at Thad and said softly, "I suggest we all run back to the ship and get out of here."

A smile spread across Thad's face. "Even if you made it to your ship, you aren't going anywhere. I've just locked out the computers. You are now my guests."

Marlene pointed a blaster at Thad. "It looks like cyborgs are as arrogant as the old holo-vids portrayed them. Unlock our computers or I'm going to put a hole through your chest the size of my fist."

Thad cocked his head to the side for a second. "Ah, I just reviewed your history since we left Earth. It appears the American military did learn a few tricks from studying our implants." He shook his head and sighed. "They created advanced soldiers with cybernetic implants and then used them as disposable tools. It's no wonder that they finally rebelled."

Lewis sighed. "Millions died during the Cyborg Wars. As a result, cybernetic research has been banned by international agreement for over 50 years."

Two women stepped out of the shadows carrying antique military M4 rifles. One of the women motioned with the barrel, and said, “Put it down slowly.”

Marlene reluctantly complied and took a step back as the other woman collected her blaster.

Thad nodded. “That’s better. All we want to do is go home, but unfortunately for you, we need your ship. I’m going to give you a better offer than your ancestors gave us. You can come with us to our homeworld or we can place you in cryosleep until more of your kind find you. At the rate of human expansion in the universe, you’ll probably only have to wait a few decades if you stay here.”

The captain shook his head. “Where my ship goes, I go.”

Thad nodded, and asked, “Do the rest of you feel the same way?”

After a few sideways glances between each other, everyone nodded.

“Then you will help us move the cryo-units to your ship. Who knows, in time you might even earn my trust.” Thad opened an access panel on the first pod and keyed in a command, and the unit lifted from the floor a few inches. He motioned Daniel over to the pod. “You take this one.”

Jason followed with the second pod. As the captain walked away pushing the third pod, Marlene leaned closer to Lewis, and whispered, “We can’t just let them take over the ship.”

Lewis shrugged. "Remember the advice you gave me when I woke up? Sometimes you just have to make the best of a bad situation."

Marlene's eyes narrowed for a second, and she abruptly turned to push her assigned cryo-pod to the ship.

Made in the USA
Columbia, SC
27 July 2024